STOWAWAY
IN A SLEIGH

Written and illustrated by C. Roger Mader

HOUGHTON MIFFLIN HARCOURT

Boston   New York

For my children,
Mary Beth, Drew, and Madeleine

The text of this book is set in Brioso.
The illustrations are pastels on paper.

Library of Congress Cataloging-in-Publication Data
Mader, C. Roger, author, illustrator.
Stowaway in a sleigh / written and illustrated by Roger Mader.
pages ; cm
Summary: Late one night, Slipper the cat awakens to find a furry-booted man in her home and,
like any curious cat would, climbs into his big red sack.
ISBN 978-0-544-48174-9
1. Cats—Juvenile fiction. [1. Cats—Fiction. 2. Santa Claus—Fiction. 3. Christmas—Fiction.] I. Title.
PZ10.3.M25St 2016
[E]—dc23
2015018705

Manufactured in China
SCP 10 9 8 7 6 5 4 3 2 1
4500599744

It was the darkest hour of night when Slipper
heard strange footsteps in the house.

Step by step on softly padded paws, she crept closer and closer.

Then she discovered . . .

. . . Mr. Furry Boots!

Slipper was smitten.

They shared a quiet moment together
before Slipper did exactly what any
curious cat would do.

Mr. Furry Boots had finished his rounds, so he
headed on home without knowing he had . . .

. . . a little passenger.

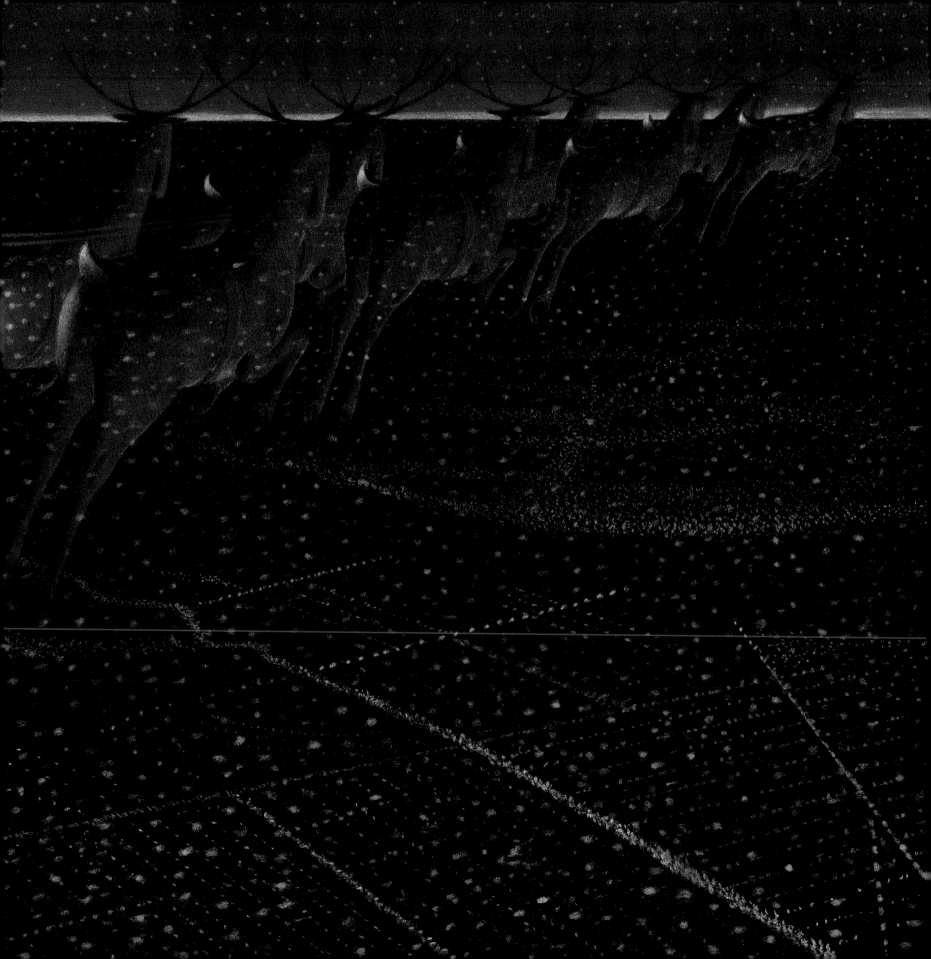

When they arrived,
Ms. Furry Boots saw
the wiggling lump.

And she let the cat out of the bag!

Slipper was all tuckered out.

The next morning she visited the room
where all the gifts are lovingly wrapped.

She found out they make toys for cats,

and made new friends.

But back at the house, Slipper
had a longing to be

home.

When Mr. Furry Boots finally found her . . .

. . . he understood.

So that night Slipper took her second ride in his sleigh, but this time she flew first class.

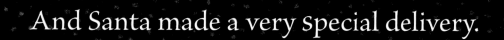
And Santa made a very special delivery.